Rainbows

By Heather Hammonds

Contents

Rainbows

Rainbows are bands of colour that form when light passes through tiny drops of water.

Rainbows are often seen in the sky after rainstorms. When the Sun comes out, sunlight shines through raindrops in the sky and this forms a rainbow.

Rainbows are made up of seven colours that always appear in the same order. They are:

■ red   ■ orange   ■ yellow   ■ green

■ blue   ■ indigo   ■ violet

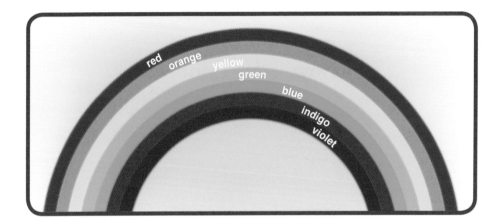

Sometimes two rainbows are seen in the sky together. When this happens, the order of colours in the second rainbow is reversed.

The different colours in a rainbow form because light enters a drop of water and then bounces back out at different angles. When the light bounces back out of the curved raindrop, different colours can be seen.

Rainbows also form in other places where there are droplets of water and sunlight.

They can be seen in the spray over waterfalls and sprinklers, and over the sea when there is spray in the air.

a moonbow

A special type of rainbow, called a moonbow, can be seen at night. The Moon has to be very bright and it needs to be raining for a moonbow to occur. Moonlight shines through drops of water in the sky.

In ancient times, people thought rainbows were made by gods, or other supernatural beings. They did not understand how rainbows were formed.

Scientists had not yet discovered that light reflects off the inside of raindrops.

Today, we know the real reason
why bands of colour form in the sky.

Rainbows form because light in the sky
bounces out of water drops at different angles.

Make a Rainbow

Goal

To prove that a rainbow forms in water droplets, in sunshine.

Materials

- a sunny day
- a shady area
- an adult's help and permission to use a hose
- a garden tap
- a hose
- a trigger nozzle for the hose
- a notebook and pencil

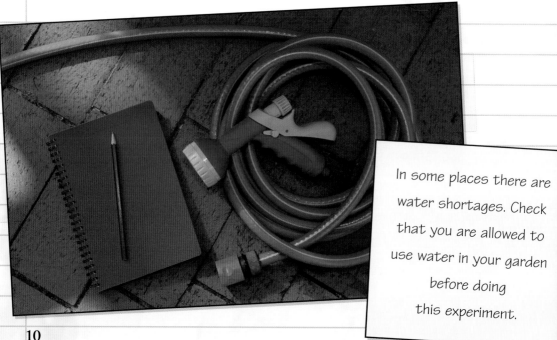

In some places there are water shortages. Check that you are allowed to use water in your garden before doing this experiment.

Steps

1. Connect one end of the hose to the garden tap.
2. Attach the trigger nozzle to the other end of the hose.

3. Turn the trigger nozzle so that the water will come out in a fine spray.
4. Turn on the tap.

5. Stand facing away from the Sun and press the trigger nozzle so a spray of water comes out.

6. Look at the ground and check for a shadow.

7. Spray the water along the shadow and try to see a rainbow.

8. Move the spray to the right and the left. Observe what happens to any rainbow that you see.

9. Take the hose into the shade, repeat steps 5–8 and try to see a rainbow.

10. Go back into the sunshine and repeat steps 5–8.

Observations

The person holding the hose in the Sun observed that a rainbow formed when water was sprayed along their shadow.

Parts of the rainbow were observed when the hose was moved from left to right.

A rainbow could not be seen in the hose spray when it was sprayed in a shady spot.

Conclusion

This experiment proves that rainbows form where there are water droplets and sunlight. They cannot form in shady areas where there is not enough sunlight.